Sam and
the Big Kids

by Emily Arnold McCully

Holiday House / New York

I LIKE TO READ is a registered trademark of Holiday House, Inc.

Copyright © 2013 by Emily Arnold McCully
All Rights Reserved
HOLIDAY HOUSE is registered in the U.S. Patent and Trademark Office.
Printed and Bound in October 2012 at Tien Wah Press, Johor Bahru, Johor, Malaysia.
The text typeface is Report School.
The artwork was created with pen and ink and watercolors.
www.holidayhouse.com
First Edition
1 3 5 7 9 10 8 6 4 2

Library of Congress Cataloging-in-Publication Data
McCully, Emily Arnold.
Sam and the big kids / by Emily Arnold McCully. — 1st ed.
p. cm. — (I like to read)
Summary: The older children tell Sam he is too small to play with them,
but when they need help Sam saves the day.
ISBN 978-0-8234-2427-6 (hardcover)
[1. Brothers and sisters—Fiction. 2. Size—Fiction.] I. Title.
PZ7.M478415Sam 2013
[E]—dc23
2011040118

The big kids were playing.

"May I play too?"
said Sam.

"You are too small,"
said his sister.
"Here is a cookie,"
said her friend.
"Go home."

"Bye-bye, Sam!"

The big kids saw
a place to hide.

"May I hide too?" said Sam.

"You are too small,"
said the friend.
"Go home."

"Look!" said the big kids.

"We can make a fort.
No one will find us here."

"May I play too?" said Sam.
"No," said the friend.
"Stay here and count to 100."

The big kids looked
for a new place.

"Wow!" said the friend.
"A boat!"

She rowed the boat.

She rowed and rowed.

She tied the boat.

98 . . . 99 . . . 100!
Sam was done.

"This is fun," his sister said.
"No one can find us now."

"Oh, no!" said the friend.
"The boat is gone!"

"Look!" said Sam's sister.
"There is Sam."
The big kids called,
"Sammy! Sammy!
Go get Mom!"

"Okay!" Sam said.

Sam ran
and ran
and ran.

"Mom!" Sam called.
"The big kids
need help!"

Sam saved the day!

I Like to Read® Books
You will like all of them!

Paperback and Hardcover
Boy, Bird, and Dog by David McPhail

Dinosaurs Don't, Dinosaurs Do by Steve Björkman

The Lion and the Mice
by Rebecca Emberley and Ed Emberley

See Me Run by Paul Meisel
A Theodor Seuss Geisel Award Honor Book

Hardcover
Car Goes Far by Michael Garland

Fish Had a Wish by Michael Garland

The Fly Flew In by David Catrow

I Have a Garden by Bob Barner

I Will Try by Marilyn Janovitz

Late Nate in a Race by Emily Arnold McCully

Look! by Ted Lewin

Mice on Ice by Rebecca Emberley
and Ed Emberley

Pig Has a Plan by Ethan Long

Sam and the Big Kids by Emily Arnold McCully

See Me Dig by Paul Meisel

Sick Day by David McPhail

You Can Do It! by Betsy Lewin

Visit holidayhouse.com to read more
about I Like to Read® Books.